Moshi monsters

Pick Your Path

The Great Googenheist

GABBY'S CAFE

SUNBIRD

Published by Ladybird Books Ltd 2012

A Penguin Company
Penguin Books Ltd, 80 Strand, London, WC2R 0RL, UK
Penguin Group (USA) Inc., 375 Hudson Street, New York 10014, USA
Penguin Books Australia Ltd, Camberwell Road, Camberwell, Victoria 3124,
Australia (A division of Pearson Australia Group Pty Ltd)
Penguin Group (NZ), 67 Apollo Drive, Rosedale, Auckland 0632,
New Zealand (a division of Pearson New Zealand Ltd)
Canada, India, South Africa

Sunbird is a trade mark of Ladybird Books Ltd

By Lauren Holowaty

www.ladybird.com

ISBN: 978-1-40939 - 087 -9
001 - 10 9 8 7 6 5 4 3 2 1
Printed in Great Britain

MOSHI MONSTERS
Pick Your Path

The Great Googenheist

3

To claim your exclusive virtual gift,
go to the sign-in page of

MOSHIMONSTERS.COM

And enter the fourth word on the second
line of the seventh page of this book!
Your surprise free gift will appear
in your treasure chest!

You're hanging out in Monstro City's Googenheim Gallery, admiring some of the most famous paintings of all time. You've heard that monsters flock from all over the world to marvel at the *Monsta Lisa,* stare open mouthed at *The Scream*, gasp in disgust at Van Goo Goo's *Sunshine Berries* and grimace at Verm-in-the-ear's, *Monster with the Worm Earring.* You just had to see it all for your very own monster-self.

After much suitable marvelling, gasping and grimacing, you decide to turn your attention to a noisy group of young Moshlings on a school visit. They're chasing each other around the Old Mouldy Masters Exhibit.

'No doubt they are about to cause extreme chaos,' you say to yourself, smiling.

Just then, you notice Fumble trip over the rope in front of the great Fablo Fiasco's monsterpiece . . . Reaching out to break his fall, the unfortunate young Moshling places his paws straight onto the painting, causing alarm bells to ring, the curator to fall off his chair, and chaos throughout the whole gallery. How bizarre, everything was turning out just as you'd predicted seconds earlier.

"Mouldy monstrous paintings! That was hilarious," you can't help chuckling. "What a clumsy little fella."

But what you didn't predict is that things were about to get worse for the poor little Moshling!

As the young Moshling is told to "move away from the painting!" by his teacher, everyone sees that the paint has come right off onto his paws, and even more shockingly, Fablo's piece now has a *missing* piece!

"How odd," you say, remembering that the painting is at least 100 years older than yourself. "How could such an old painting be wet after all this time?"

The Moshling bursts into Potion Ocean floods of tears, as all his classmates are in fits of gurgling giggles. You can't help feeling really sorry for him.

"What's going on here, then?" says a curator, arriving on the scene, wearing a Fake Tash and trying to look and sound like the infamous Inspector Clueless.

On closer inspection, the curator notices that the Googenheim's entire collection of Old Mouldy Masters has been replaced with forgeries. They're gunky and wet, and there seem to be a few little things that don't seem right. Although they look pretty much exactly like the originals, the paint looks like it's made of something, really quite strange, but no one seems to be sure what it is.

"Someone must have taken the original paintings," you say, "but who, and why, and how much could one of those mouldy old pictures be worth anyway?"

"Zillions of Rox!" the curator immediately replies,

fake moustache whiskers twitching, "and without these historical artifacts, the Googenheim will have to close its glassy doors – the whole of the Monst-art world will never be the same again!"

Suddenly, you hear shouts of "Ooh la la!" from Monst-art critics up and down Ooh La Lane, over and over again.

'So,' you think to yourself, with your own detective inspector's head on, 'is this some anti-art un-installation from Art Lee, where he has taken the masters underground to the Underground Tunnels? Perhaps Bug and Ratty have been up to their usual museum mischief? Maybe Sly Chance has been wheelin' and dealin' in art to make some quick Rox, or Mizz Snoots has taken selling extravagant items at Horrods to this extreme? Or has the Master of Scientific genius and former Sinister Minister, Dr Strangeglove been up to some hand or glove painting himself? He did always seem to be hanging around outside the Googenheim after all.'

So many questions, so much chaos. It's a complete Fablo Fiasco and it seems Monstro City needs you to sort it out! The future of the Googenheim and its famous paintings is now in **your** paws! You must solve the mystery of the Great Googenheist, before the evil paint dries!

If you see some paw-prints along the wall and decide to follow them out of the gallery, **turn to page 28.** They have to be those of the art thief or someone up to something, and you have to be hot on their Moshi tails!

7

If you decide to search the Googenheim for more clues, **turn to page 40.** The paw-prints could be some of the school group just messing around and you want to be totally informed before you head anywhere.

You follow the light in the distance for what feels like an eerily long time, but for some reason it seems to be getting dimmer, rather than brighter. You're not sure where you are, but it's dark, damp and not a place you want to hang around in for long, not long at all. Maybe you've stumbled on a secret underground escape tunnel for the art thief? But the further you go, it's beginning to seem just as likely that you have simply walked into some sort of storage space for old paintings.

Realising you can no longer see any footprints, so you're not really sure why you opted to go this way, and that this is probably not getting you any closer at all to the whereabouts of the thief, you decide to head back. You turn around and . . .

"Aaarrgghh!" you scream, as what you can only imagine is a gang of rebel, bigger-than-usual Spookies Moshlings, jump out straight in front of you. You can just about make out the shapes of a Woolly Blue Hoodoo, a Fancy Banshee, a Furry Heebee and a scarier than usual Baby Ghost.

You turn back around and race away from the gang as fast as you can towards the dim light, huffing and puffing all the way and just a teeny tiny bit scared.

"BANG!"

"Ouch!" you cry, hitting a hard wall. It's a dead end. **"Yuck,"** you grimace, as your face is covered in some sort of glow in the dark algae that seems to be losing its strength.

"So, that's what the dim light was," you sigh, a little disappointed that you seem to have made a bad choice.

Realising that the Spookies are only Moshlings after all, and nothing really to be all that scared of, you head back the way you came, until you are back at the entrance of the two tunnel openings.

"This time, I'll go right!" you decide.

Turn to page 54.

The more you think about it, the more you're totally convinced that Art Lee must have had something to do with the stolen paintings. Not because he wanted to sell them, but because of his need to de-face the Old Masters and make some sort of statement, without causing zillions of Rox worth of damage. It was his way of breaking away from the oldness and mouldiness of Main (and Sludge) Street art, and creating something new and exciting for Monstro City.

"That's probably why the paw-prints were attracting so many young Moshlings," you say. "They're impressionable and fed up with the old and the mouldy. These new paintings and paint are more exciting to them."

You're not entirely sure what Lee's statement is trying to say, why he didn't just literally 'say' it, or where he may have hidden the original paintings, but you do know that you have to find him to find out the answers.

You exit the gallery through the main doors and not the gift shop.

"No time for souvenirs today!" you cry.

Bursting through the doors, you have your monstrous mind on the mission at hand: heading into the Underground Tunnels to find Art Lee. You know that it's going to be hard, as no one really knows exactly what Lee looks like from the front (he's only really been seen from the back and in the distance). But you're determined to find a way.

You find the nearest entrance to the Underground Tunnels and head deep, deep down.

"Weeeee!" you cry, sliding down an extremely muddy and slippery slope into the underground world.

As you trudge through the sludge, you keep an eye out (well it just popped out by mistake really) for signs of Art Lee's presence. The walls seem quite bare and dark, until you turn the corner . . .

"Ooooh, colours!" you gasp, almost blinded by an explosion of blues, reds and Sunshine Berry yellows. "Pretty!"

You never did get to see Lee's infamous '*Popp-it with Bobbing Balloons*' piece, because everyone had done what the title had told them and popped it all before you'd arrived. But this was something else! It is graffiti like you have never seen before, and it makes you want to paint, too!

"Well, hello there," you hear a voice say, but you can't actually see anyone or work out where it is coming from. Perhaps because you were almost blinded by the colourful work of art. "Please join us, and paint."

You can just about make out a few brushes and paints in front of you, so you do as the mystery voice says, bend down to pick them up, and . . .

"Et voila!" And just like that, you have created your very own monster-piece on the wall!

"This is so much fun, I could do this forever!" And little do you know that's exactly what you will be doing forever more! You have unleashed your inner contemporary artist and just can't stop. You paint piece after piece, but you're still hungry for more.

Now, there is no exit through anywhere. You are lost in the underground art world, never to be seen again . . .

Turn to page 71.

You drink a very little sip of the Eye C U Goo Smoothie. Even the teeny tiny little bit tastes absolutely disgusting.

"Huh per!" you spit it out all over the floor.

You try to take another sip, but you just can't.

"Oh well," you sigh, giving up. "Maybe I should head to the Googenheim and see what's going on there instead."

Back at the gallery, you find crowds of Moshis.

"What's going on?" you ask the Poppet next to you.

"I'm not sure," she answers, "but it seems the Moshlings have been found in some sort of cave with Strangeglove."

"I see," you say, about to ask more, when an over-eager Zommer cuts in. Out of breath and trying to get as many words out as possible, he says:

"Puff, Moshlings, puff, puff, hypnotized in Fun Park dream world, puff, Strangeglove, puff, trap to glump them, puff, puff, but Super Moshis, puff, puff, need help to stop him, puff, puff."

Between the huffs and puffs you gather that your help is needed, so you weave through the crowd to the front and spot a very high bridge through the mass of fog. You feel like the bridge is beckoning you towards it, with a sign saying, 'Over here!', but you're not sure how you can get up onto it.

Suddenly, you remember your shopping from the Bizarre Bazaar. "My Yellow Jelly Floor!" you cry. You roll out the floor and use it to jump up high onto the bridge. Then you leap into a Hot Smelly-Air Balloon and are transported to a cave in the Moshi Fun Park.

"Strangeglove!" you yell at the top of your voice, spotting him as soon as you enter the cave.

He looks over at you confused as to who you are and where in Monstro City you could have possibly come from. While Strangeglove is distracted, a group of Super Moshis are able to sneak up, grab him and move him far away from the controls of his glumping machine, saving all the Moshlings from their doom!

After a good night's rest, the next day you feel very proud. And so you should, it may have been an accident, and Strangeglove had managed to run off, but your resourcefulness and perfect timing played an essential part in saving the Moshlings **and** the Googenheim's art collection.

THE END

You find a big rubber stopper and work as quickly as you can, pressing it into the end of test tube 'A'.

"Phewee!" you sigh, relieved, as everything seems to calm down.

But it seems you sighed too soon, goon! The mixture is now bubbling and fizzing more than ever before! What are you going to do now? You scramble to reach the power source, but . . .

BANG!!!

****

The next day you find yourself in the safety of your own bed, but because of your exposure to all the Eye C U Goo that covered you, furry head to toe, you are now permanently hypnotized! And just to add to insult to injury, for some reason you keep trying to climb up your walls over and over again! The doctors say you may never recover, but that since the Super Moshis have found Strangeglove and stopped him from glumping the Moshlings, they are now all on the case to find you an antidote!

THE END

SPLASH!!!!

Uh oh, what have you done? That obviously was not the right button to press. All the screens are flashing up, "Abort! Abort!" and the train seems to be falling into a big ... blue ... watery ... grave ...

"Noooooo!!!" you cry out, frantically pressing the orange button.

You're only in a training simulator, so you're fine, but you hear Elder Furi's voice say,

"I'm afraid this is the very (wet) end of *your* Super Moshi career, young one!"

THE END

You set the Colorama paint pots and blaster cannons to every blue option you possibly can, crank them up to the max and stand there, ready to be blue-eyed, blue bushy-tailed and blue-bodied forever! Or at least until you find the art thief and can come back for an almighty wash!

"PWWFF, WHOOSH, PANG!" gasps the machine, completely overloaded with all that blue. You are given not just a simple old grandmother Moshi's blue rinse, but a bodaciously blue tornado is blasted at you from every angle and it tastes not dissimilar to the gunk at the Googenheim.

When the blue blasters finally grind to a halt, you give yourself a blue-dry with the fur dryer and head to the mirror to see yourself, looking top to tail blue-tastic!

"That should just about do it!" you cheer. "Now all I have to do is find someone who matches me, with the exact same colour combination. Then I will have found the art thief who left their grubby blue paw prints all over the Googenheim! I'll be able to track down the missing paintings, return them to the gallery and be the hero of all of Monstro City! My name will go down in history as the Greatest Googenheist Mystery Solver of All Time . . . or something perhaps just a little bit catchier than that! I'm sure Roary Scrawl at the *Daily Growl* will think of something better."

Feeling pretty pleased with yourself and ready for fame, you go to leave the Colorama Workshop. But just as you get to the door, a team of Super Moshis appears to stop you in your blue mist!

"The thief!" cries Super Zommer, swooping his cape around and swishing his paw straight at you.

"No, you don't understand . . ." you begin, backing away from them, and trying to explain at the same time.

But the Super Moshis aren't listening.

"You're absolutely covered in evidence," pitches in Super Poppet. "There's no denying that."

"But, I . . ."

"No excuses," interrupts Super Zommer. "You look and smell just like the gunk all over the Googenheim and the gunk in the forged paintings."

Super Furi comes closer towards you and, using a paw to pluck some of your fur off, feels it, listens to its crackling noise and then licks it.

'Gross!' you think to yourself.

"Yep, same texture, sound and taste too. This is definitely the same stuff!"

"I know it's the same stuff," you try one last time, "I discovered all those things using my investigative senses at the gallery and I've been trying to re-create . . ."

"Aha!" cries Super Zommer, cutting you off again. "We've caught the art thief totally 'blue-handed'!"

"Ha, ha, ho, ho, ho!" chuckle the team together, exploding into fits of giggles. "Blue-handed! Love it!" They'd obviously been waiting to say that line for quite some time!

You back up further and further away from the Super

Moshis and onto the painting platform.

"Right then!" shouts Super Zommer. "Put your paws up!"

Scared of being surrounded and realising they aren't going to listen to what you have to say, you slowly reach for the sky, as they say in the smoovies.

"Now, put one leg up!" screams Super Poppet.

So, balancing one leg in the air carefully, you desperately try not to fall over.

"And hop to the left!" shouts Super Furi.

"Then, shake your bootie!" sings Super Diavlo.

You soon realize that the Super Moshis are having fun with you again, and are making you 'Do The Funky Monster'! But you are at their mercy, so do as they say, and once again the team explodes into laughter. They laugh so much that they end up on their backs, with their arms and legs in the air!

"Perhaps this is my time to make a run for it and escape?" you whisper to yourself, quietly.

"What was that?" one of the Super Moshis asks, overhearing.

"Or maybe I should use the blasters on them?" you say, this time completely to yourself and ignoring the question.

So what's it to be, Detective Moshi? The choice is yours.

If you decide to make a run for it, while the Super Moshis are still on their backs in hysterics, **turn to page 38.**

If you decide to use the Colorama's colour blasters to spray the Super Moshis and distract them even more, **turn to page 61.**

Convinced Bug and Ratty are at the bottom of all this, you race back through the tunnel in search of the dynamic duo. Zooming through the galleries, with your eyes peeled (not literally, that would be gross!) you survey the place for signs of buginess and ratiness, but find nothing.

As you get to the exit, you see what looks like a Mystery Box. You pick it up, thinking it could be a clue, turn the handle and a scary Jack-in-the-Box springs out and bites you on the nose! "Well at least I'm on the right bug and rat's tail!" you chuckle, trying to hide your pain.

You follow a trail of joke boxes all with different traps that seem to have been left for you. As you come across each one, you are careful not to touch them or turn the handles, but still you are attacked: chattering wind-up, Katpire teeth and Vampy's Fangs gnaw their way through the boxes and Fly Trap Salads tempt your taste buds, then bite you back. It's just one big nibbling nightmare!

After the 100th joke box, it dawns on you that you've been sent on a massive and very wild rat and bug chase all over Monstro City, and you're not getting anywhere, fast! Plus, you're running out of places on your body to be bitten!

"Bug and Ratty are jokers, not thieves. What's funny about stealing paintings? They must have made me think they were, and that's their joke!"

Really, you should have known better. The joke has been on you all this time! Maybe you should trace your steps back and start at the beginning again?

THE END

You zoom back to the Googenheim where you started this somewhat eventful day, and head straight up to the gallery to observe.

As you get there, you find it hard to breath, as the room is full of a colourful mist coming from the forged paintings. It smells very similar to some of the gases from your experiments in the lab earlier and your vision becomes very hazy.

Through the fogginess, you can just about spy the pre-historic tails of a group of cute little Dino Moshlings, disappearing around the corner.

You tip-toe towards them, as quietly as you can, and see them crawling through some sort of little trap door with a little sign on it saying 'this way to your dream world!' The trap door is under an enormous bridge, with another sign saying, 'or this way if you prefer'.

"I don't remember seeing that here before," you say, confused. "It's almost like it's a mirage or a hologram. But then, how can I see it as well as the Moshlings? I'm not hypnotized, am I?"

You want to keep following the Dinos, but you are far too big to crawl through the miniature trap door, and far too small to be able to jump over the bridge!

All you can do is watch and know that the Moshlings are heading towards Strangeglove's trap and probably their eventual doom . . .

Just then, you have a brain wave, and remember what you picked up earlier from Bizarre Bazaar.

"My Yellow Jelly Floor!" you gasp.

You lay the floor down and, with a wibbly wobbly run-up, use it to help you bounce up high and land on top of the bridge.

Standing on the bridge, you feel yourself being pushed into some sort of Hot Smelly-Air Balloon, powered (in part) by gas from Roland Jones' Wobble Ade burps. It carries you over Monstro City and far away, and drops you off in what appears to be the Moshi Fun Park.

"This looks like absolute paradise for Moshlings!" you say, smiling. But then you realize you must keep your wits about you and find Strangeglove. The place is enormous, so where do you start?

If you decide to follow the biggest group of Moshlings, **turn to page 50.**

If you join the Moshlings on the Ferris Wheel, you'll get a nice aerial view of the park to spot Strangeglove from up there, **turn to page 58.**

Continuing your journey down Main Street and ignoring Sly Chance, as he's probably up to something dodgy and you don't want anything to do with it, you keep a look out for anything else suspicious.

You pop into Bizarre Bazaar and see if Bushy Fandango has any treasures from her latest trip to the Yappalation Mountains. Something might make useful equipment for your search for the art thief.

"Good day," says Bushy, greeting you. "Monsters are my business and business is good! Now, what can I get you?"

You stare up at the shelves, looking for detective-type stuff.

"Purple Eyes Wallpaper." That would be great for keeping lots of eyes on things, but you could hardly wallpaper the streets with it!

"A Yellow Bowler Ball, nope. A Cuddly Human, nope . . . Eau de Trash Perfume by Zack Binspin . . . now that could be useful."

You also purchase a F-f-funky Door. It says it can 'bend time and space' so this could definitely come in handy. Then finally you pop a Yellow Jelly Floor in your backpack, just in case you have to wobble and bounce your way to the other side of somewhere, at some point.

"Thanks, Bushy," you say and you continue to walk along Main Street. Trying not to go the usual route, just in case anyone is following you, you sneak past the Timernator, picking up your stride, and turn left down

towards Sludge Street, past the EN-GEN Room. You take a moment to wave to Dizzee Bolt, the Chief EN-GENeer, as you know her well from your Thursday night Ju-don't Martial Arts class.

Reaching the Games Starcade, you spot Max Volume and ask him for directions to the Volcano. But you don't think he can hear you over the noise of his enormous Boom Box, **"BOOM, BOOM, BOOM!"**

You watch in awe as he does a crazy dance, finishing with an outrageously brain bedazzling head spin!

You look at him more closely, wondering how he does it, and then you notice that his arms, legs and head are all pointing and facing the same direction, towards . . .

"The Volcano!" you cry, seeing the smoking mountain in the distance. "Thanks Max, my man!"

You walk on by, past the Dodgy Dealz shack and over the hills towards the enormous volcano, which you can't believe you hadn't spotted before! Over the hills and far away, alive with the sound of the rushing lava, getting louder and louder, you trample on until you reach the base.

"Now what?" you ask, unsure of how to actually enter the Volcano.

"Need some help?" asks a Moshi hanging around nearby, wearing a red cape.

'That must be one of those Super Moshis,' you think to yourself.

"I'm looking for Elder Furi," you say.

"Follow me," says the kind Moshi.

If you decide to ignore the Moshi in the cape and find your own way, **turn to page 77.**

If you decide to go with the Moshi in the cape, **turn to page 33.**

You've always loved a game of eyes-pie, so you race over to the mucky paw-prints on the wall and begin using the usual investigative measures detectives use. You look for clues as to who the dastardly art thief might be, using your five monster senses . . .

First, you observe the situation using your eyes. You stare long and hard at the prints and notice that they appear to be mainly blue, but you're not really sure how, as they seem to be changing colour. You also note that they have indeed been made by some sort of monster paw, or glove.

"So much for being hot on the thief's heels, this is more like being hot on the thief's hands!" you laugh. The prints seem to be everywhere, all over the walls, floor and ceiling, going in every direction around the gallery, and every which way you look.

"It's amazing how many prints there are," you gasp, trying to take it all in, but beginning to feel like some sort of Goggle Eyed Wall Trout.

Completely unsure of which trail to follow and whether to trust what you think you are seeing with your very own (now very goggly) eyes, you decide your next plan must be to use your keen sense of smell. That way, you'll soon be able to sniff out the thief's scent. Your incredible nose always 'nose' how to sniff out more clues, and it's not let you down in the past.

"Maybe I'll find something that has been under my very nose all this time," you say.

So you place your schnozzle closer and closer to the paint until you're rubbing your nose well and truly in it . . .

"Ah... ah... ah... ah-chooooooo!" You sneeze your biggest sneeze ever, as if you have just tried to wolf down an enormous bag of Pepper Popcorn!

"Well, that part of the investigation took a bit of a nose dive. Maybe I should try something else," you say, wiping your somewhat snotty hands on your knees, hoping that no one 'nose' what you're doing. Feeling the sticky snottiness makes you think of your next plan of action.

"SPLAT!" you shove your hand into one of the gunky prints, hoping its texture will give you some clues as to where it came from. The consistency is thick and gloopy, just like Gloop Soup and it gets stickety stuck on to your hand.

"It feels as though we have a bit of a sticky situation here," you say.

"Cackle, spleet, cackle!" says the gloopy paint gunk.

You raise your hand to your ear to listen in very carefully to what it might say next, but your hand gets stuck to your ear and you soon realize you're up to your Broccoli Sp'-ears in it! Prising your hand away from your ear, you try to lick the gunk off with your tongue, to get it off of your hand.

"This stuff tastes crazier than a Hypnololly!" you cry, remembering back to the time when you ignored the warning on the packet and had so many lollies you

quacked like a duck for a whole month! You know you've tasted something similar to this before, but you can't put your tongue on it.

"Maybe if I just taste a little bit more, I'll remember?" you say, and soon enough you find yourself stuffing your face full of the gunk.

"Ah-ha! That's it!" you cry, remembering why it was familiar. "The Colorama Workshop." Last time you were there you opted for a full purplelicious makeover and accidentally opened your mouth. This tasted just like it! Perhaps if you ate the whole trail you'd find the thief and also find somewhere to buy more of this delicious new sweetness?

If you want to eat more, and more, and more, and keep following the trail of prints, **turn to page 48.** After all, Handsmell and Grottel made it to the witch's cottage this way, didn't they?

If you decide the weird, yet yummy painty prints can only be from one place, head to the Port and continue your investigations at the Colorama Workshop and **turn to page 68**.

Shaking off the remnants of the Toad Soda episode or epi-soda, as it should be named, you continue along the tunnel and it starts to get wider and wider, and lighter and lighter.

Soon, you find yourself in some sort of reading room and it's a little like you imagine Roary Scrawl's writer's office to be like. There are books and newspapers everywhere you turn, as well as a few interesting objects on the table.

"I must have found the Googenheim's underground Hiss-story of Art Research Room," you cry, very pleased with yourself.

You head over to the table and find some Reading Glasses. They are very useful as monsters read words from the inside out. There is also an Actual-Magnifying Glass for magically making things actually and literally bigger than they really are, and finally a TOP SECRET file containing a list of the Googenheim's paintings and how much they are worth, and other secret things.

"These things could all come in very handy!" you say, "very handy indeed."

Heading back to the gallery with your newfound equipment, you ignore the trick Rox on the floor, and watch out for anything about to pounce, jump out, trip you over, or generally play some sort of joke on you. With your silliness senses on red alert, you make it back through unscathed.

"Ha, ha!" you laugh triumphantly, reaching the Googenheim's entranceway. But you laugh too soon, as

just as you spy the crowds of people, a random Bouffant Wig comes flying towards you, as if from nowhere. It tickles you on the nose and you can't stop sneezing for a whole ten minutes!

Eventually recovering from your embarrassing sneeze, you head up to the main gallery, which, as you seem to have broken the sign from swinging on it, is now simply labelled 'The Scene of the Grime' handwritten on a scrappy old piece of torn paper.

When you get up there, you take a look at your new tools to see if they can help you with your investigation. The Reading Glasses and the Actual-Magnifying Glass would be great for looking into the paint on the forgeries and the paw prints left on the wall, but the TOP SECRET file tells you some of the shops wanting to sell the paintings.

So what will you decide to do first?

If you decide to take a closer look at the prints in the gallery, **turn to page 64.**

If you decide to head to the shops to search for the missing paintings, **turn to page 79.**

"OK," you say, following on behind the stranger.

He takes you along a rocky track and around the base of the Volcano.

"I thought the Super Moshi Headquarters were inside the Volcano?" you say, but you don't get an answer.

You're led into a little cave. Inside is a treasure trove of capes, masks and costumes.

'This is a very strange place for an HQ,' you say to yourself. 'Maybe it's where the Super Moshis get dressed?'

"So, what will it be? Purple with a yellow star, or blue with a flash?" asks the stranger pointing towards the capes.

"I thought all the Super Moshis wore red capes?" you ask, but he just ignores you.

Just then it dawns on you.

'This is a trap and this so-called Super Moshi is a decoy!' you think. 'He must be working for Strangeglove!'

You keep up the pretence that you have been sucked in by the Moshi's games for a while, but then, faking a trip to the bathroom, you race to Moshi HQ and inform them of the trickster. The Super Moshis immediately pick him up and take him to the Volcano for questioning.

Your picture is in the *Daily Growl* the next day, and the story of how you cleverly tracked down one of Strangeglove's secret henchmen makes headline news. Even though you didn't exactly solve the crime, at least you played your part in the battle against the evil Strangeglove and became famous overnight!

THE END 33

You blow out the flame on the burner, thus removing the power source, and immediately, all the fizzing and banging in the conical flask seems to cease to a halt. All that listening in science class must have paid off!

"Phewee!" you gasp, wiping the sweat off of your brow, neck, armpits and hands. "Flaming test tubes, that was close!"

"Now then," you say, remembering your conundrum before all the fizzing in the flask, "I need to work out what happens when the Moshlings get hypnotized and where it leads them."

Just then, you and the rest of the lab-coated Super Moshis hear Elder Furi's voice above you:

"Greetings, Super Moshis. I have an important announcement to make," he begins. "We have been notified by hidden sources that hundreds of Moshlings have been going missing since the events at the Googenheim. This problem has now escalated to a CODE BERRY RED ALERT and we need your help!"

"I was right!" you gasp. "Moshlings are the targets of this grimy crime."

"All Super Moshis must report to HQ immediately," continues Elder Furi.

You're not sure what a Code Berry Red Alert is, but it sounds important, so you whip off your lab coat and race to the centre of the Volcano. When you get there you are surrounded by hundreds of Super Moshis, all eager to see how they can help.

"You must use everything in your power to find out where the Moshlings are being taken."

You think carefully about what you could do to help. Before all this happened you were going to try to hypnotize yourself with the Eye C U Goo, so you too could go to the place where the Moshlings are being taken. Maybe this was how you could help out? Surely no one else would be willing to hypnotize themselves?

"Or I could try heading back to the Googenheim and make some observations?"

You're completely bamboozled, flummoxed and confused. What should you do this time? No pressure, but the consequences may mean everything to the lives of hundreds of Moshlings!

If you decide to hypnotize yourself to find the Moshlings, **turn to page 75.**

If you head back to the scene of the crime at the Googenheim, **turn to page 23.**

You saunter over to Sly, as casually as you can.

He quickly hides all of his arms behind his back. "What can I do for you?" he asks.

"Well," you begin. "I'm looking for something to brighten up my walls. Something with a bit of historical value."

"How much do ya wanna spend?" asks Sly.

"Zillions of Rox," you reply.

Sly looks at you, as if you would never be able to get your paws on that many Rox.

"Err . . . err . . . I just won the Monstro Snottery!" you explain.

"You should've said earlier," Sly says. Completely taken in by your deception, he pulls out lots of Old Mouldy Masters paintings!

"Aha!" you cry. "Gotcha. I'm afraid I'm an undercover spy looking for stolen paintings and YOU are coming with ME!"

"But these aren't . . ."

"Don't say a word!" you cry, not letting Sly explain, and swiftly escorting him to the Googenheim.

"I'm afraid you've been mistaken," the curator says. "These are knock-offs of the real paintings."

"More forgeries!" you gasp. "Stinking rubbish!"

"Hey, don't knock my knock-offs," replies Sly, a little hurt. "They make me a lot of money!"

But the curator is actually really pleased.

"Sly should not be selling knock-offs at all. It has been

costing the Googenheim thousands of Rox in potential shop sales for years," the curator explains to you. "Well done, detective Moshi! We can now put a stop to this."

You may not have solved the crime of the art thief, but you have accidentally discovered lots of other art crimes instead!

THE END

Leaping over the laughing Super Moshis like a Ninja Moshling in combat, you reach the door of the Colorama Workshop, escape, and without turning back, race all the way to the safety of your house, as fast as you can.

"Phew! I made it!" you gasp, out of breath, eventually arriving at your door. "Home sweet home! And what a day it has been!"

But as you walk inside, things seem a little different from usual. Your once very colourful house is now entirely blue!

You find yourself completely surrounded by Sky Blue and Blue Swirl Wallpaper and the whole place smells of the Essence of Blue – squeezed from the bluest berries on the bluest bushes in the bluest part of Monstro City. You look in your Blue Mirror and see that you totally match your house.

You decide that enough is enough and you must wash your blues away!

"Perhaps, I'll start with a good old scrub-a-dub-dub in the shower?" you cry. But all your scrubbing and dubbing just won't wash the blue off. Drying yourself off and rubbing your eyes with a Blue Beach Towel, you realize that you must have overdone it at the Colorama Workshop and given yourself permanent blue vision!

Nice and clean, but still very, very blue, you fling on your Blue Jeans, Bright Blue Sneakers, Blue Cat Beanie Hat, Patterned Blue Shawl and Blue Feather Boa for a touch of glamour.

"I must go back to the Workshop," you cry. But it soon dawns on you that you can't go back – the Super Moshis would catch you. In fact you daren't leave the house again. You, my dear true blue Moshi, are a wanted criminal!

Staring out of your Curvy Blue Window, you feel like a prisoner inside your own blue home. You're stuck in your very own version of Fablo Fiasco's blue period, never able to show your blue face again. You decide to wallow completely in the Monster Blues and pump up some Blues music on your (Blue) Big Bad Boom Box.

"Maybe I should have stayed in the gallery and searched for more clues," you sigh.

But, it's not so bad really. Blue is your favourite colour after all. Well, it has to be now, anyway, whether you like it or not!

THE END

"Something rather odd seems to be going on here," you say in your most suspicious detective-like voice, mimicking your idol Inspector Clueless. You begin your search around the Googenheim, determined to find out who the art thief is.

First, you inspect all the paintings in the Old Mouldy Masters Exhibit, and very carefully feel that they are all indeed wet, just like Fablo Fiasco's monsterpiece.

"I shall conclude that the naughty thief must have done this today," you gather cleverly, "or else the paint would be dry by now."

You suspect that the culprit may still be on the premises, or at least not long gone, so you begin to look in every nook and cranny.

"Nothing can get past me!" you cry, as a hoard of young Moshlings race right by you, whilst you are staring aimlessly at some silly little nook in a corner!

Just as you are about to head to the next room, you look down at your hands and notice that a little bit of each painting you touched is stuck to them. It has a slight shine to it, unlike any paint you have ever seen before. Despite thinking these may well be the perfect souvenirs for your day out, you decide that a postcard of the *Monsta Lisa* for your mum would be better.

Then you start to worry, thinking to yourself, 'What if somebody sees I have this paint on my hands? I don't want anyone to think that I have something to do with painting the forgeries.'

So as quickly as you can, you head to the bathroom to wash your hands, constantly looking around you to make sure no one is looking. Again, you manage to miss a hoard of visitors race by you; Sly Chance, Art Lee and Bug and Ratty!

Whilst you're in the bathroom, you notice they have a shower. You're about due your annual wash, so decide to take the plunge and strip off, leaving your clothes hanging on a hook. That way you'll get rid of any evidence that may link you to the paint in the forgeries and ultimately the grimey crime itself.

"La, la, la-la, la, la!" you sing to yourself in the shower.

You dry off and reach for your clothes. Then you reach further and further, but there is nothing to reach for. All of your clothes have disappeared and only your shoes have been left behind.

"Wandering wardrobes!" you cry. "Where are my clothes?"

You exit the bathroom and continue your investigations like a true professional, despite being annoyed about your clothes.

Suddenly something catches your eye, so you head to the slope that goes down to the entrance of the Googenheim. At the top of the slope, you look down just in time to see that you are stepping on a banana skin and . . .

"WHOOAAHHH!" you slide all the way down the polka-dotted slope. Just before you reach the bottom where a whole crowd of Moshis and Moshlings have gathered,

you reach up and grab onto the 'Gallery' sign and swing from it, Indiana Bones style.

"Phewee!" you gasp.

"Hooray!" cheers the crowd.

Whilst you're swinging from the roof rafters, you notice some footprints on the red carpet leading to the Googenheim's Hall of Fame.

'I'm never gonna be able to get through the crowd to check out those footprints,' you think to yourself, 'unless . . .'

Hooking your feet up over the sign, you give yourself enough momentum for one enormous swing that takes you over the heads of the crowd. There are a few literal close shaves where the rough parts of your Skullmunster Sneakers get a little too close to a few taller than average Zommers, and take the tips off their crazy spikey hair-doos and don'ts. But other than that, you're all good.

The Art Challenge Judges say it's a ten for artistic style (as you fly through the air you take time to check your reflection in the window), ten for use of colour (your face is extremely red) and ten for overall originality (no one has ever seen anyone do anything quite this extreme to get to the Hall of Fame before).

You almost nail your landing (you land on one foot, wobble around all over the place and fall over twice, but eventually stand proud as if nothing ever happened), and you find yourself right underneath the sparkly gold Hall of Fame sign. Once again, you gasp "Phewee!" and the crowd cheers, "Hooray!"

"Ta-dah!" You're hoping for another cheer, but the crowd is distracted by a Furi nearby, stamping his feet for attention, and they seem to have forgotten all about you.

"Oh well," you say. "At least my fans will leave me in peace to continue my investigation."

You follow the prints along the red carpet, bowing for your (now imaginary), adoring fans as you go. You like pretending you're Simon Growl's hottest new contestant for the Monster Factor.

Finding yourself in a dark room, you feel your way around you to find out where to go next. You can just about see there are two little tunnel openings on each side of you. One to the left, and one to the right . . .

If you decide to go left, **turn to page 9.**

If you decide to go right, **turn to page 54.**

SKEERREECH! The train screeches to a halt, just on the edge of the bank that leads down into the depths of Potion Ocean.

"Phewee!" you gasp, relieved. "That was close."

You're so close to the water's edge in fact, you must be very careful not to make any sudden moves that may tip the train over the edge.

Shuffling along like a Stunt Penguin, you make your way to the back of the driver's carriage, trying to keep your weight equally balanced, whilst also trying to keep an eye on Strangeglove to make sure he doesn't make a run for it . . .

SPLASH!! Make that 'swim' for it! You watch Strangeglove as he dives into the water and starts to monster paddle away as fast as he can.

Three more options flash up on the screen. Reluctantly and nervously you tiptoe back to the front of the carriage, trying hard not to make it tip, and read what it says.

'Gift Island Ferry, Colonel's Flutterby Net or Duster of Destiny.'

"I must think fast," you say, hearing the train creak and creak further and further forward. "No time to start up the ferry, no sneezing needed this time, so it has to be:

"Go, Colonel's Flutterby Net!" you demand. The net comes out ahead of you and catches Strangeglove mid-stroke, flinging him up into the air and back onto dry land with a SPLAT!

Suddenly, you hear a fanfare! **"De, de, de, de, de,**

dah, dah!"

"Well done, young train-ee Super Moshi," you hear Elder Furi's voice say from a speaker above you. "You have passed your train-in with flying doctors!"

You're very pleased with yourself for passing the train-in, but your nerves are wrecked and you've been put off being a Super Moshi for life.

"It's just too nerve racking," you say, "I think I'll leave it to the experts!"

You say goodbye to all at HQ and head on home for a nice relaxing evening, listening to Hair-o-Sniff Unplugged on your Furry Luv Chair . . .

"Solving one mystery today is enough for me," you sigh, contentedly.

THE END

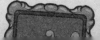

You are led to a secret Super Moshi research lab.

Inside you are surrounded by coloured potions in test tubes. They are bubbling and boiling away, like the waters of Bubblebath Bay.

"Bubble, bubble, splurt, splurt, sprrrr . . . FIZZ! POP!"

A hologram projection of Elder Furi explains to you that they believe Dr Strangeglove is indeed the art thief, as you suspected. They just need to prove it as quickly as they can, in order to find out where he is and stop him from doing any more evil. Tamara Tesla has taken some samples from the scene of the grime at the Googenheim, and you have been chosen to help them investigate.

"Poten-tious potions!" you gasp, excitedly, as you put on your scientific genius lab coat and goggles.

"We think the 'paint' used in the forgeries is a very rare substance called, 'Eye C U Goo'," continues Elder Furi, "and that some of its ingredients contain HOIRCG."

"HOIRCG?" you ask, confused.

"Hypnotizing Optical Illusion Rainbow Coloured Gunk," says Elder Furi, as if it was obvious! "We just have some last experiments to do, to break down the properties, so we can find the source and work out Strangeglove's whereabouts."

You are to carry out some tests on who the gunk attracts the most. You set to work with your equipment and your results tell you that Moshlings in particular are attracted to the goo and are easily hypnotized by it.

"Of course, it all makes sense. This must be a cunning experiment to trap Moshlings!" you gasp. Strangeglove must've stolen the original Old Mouldy Master collection and replaced them with his own handiwork. The Moshlings stare at the paintings and are hypnotized by the Eye C U Goo. They see the trail of glove prints made of the strange goo and it entices them to follow it like zombies.

"Now, if I could only work out where the hypnotizing is taking them . . ." you say, realizing you have a big conundrum.

"Should I try hypnotizing myself with the Eye C U Goo? Or . . ."

But you don't have time to do anything, as your conical flask is fizzing and banging, and you need to take control before it explodes!

"Now, I can either put a plug at the end of tube 'A' to contain it," you say, "or I could try disconnecting the power source, by blowing out the flame on the burner."

So what will it be, scientific genius?

If you decide to use the plug, **turn to page 16.**

If you decide to disconnect the power,
turn to page 34.

47

"Scrumplelicious!" you cry, continuing to scoff down the entire trail of prints, as quickly as you can. The dining experience is an explosion of all your favourite flavours rolled into one. It's as loud as a sizeable chunk of Roarberry Cheesecake, as gunky as Slopcorn and as crunchy as Quenut Butter.

Just as you think you are getting closer to gobbling up all of the prints, suddenly you begin to feel like you are spinning round and round like a Backwards Puzzle Clock.

"Is this a wind up?" you ask, wondering whether you have been unknowingly put on the new Moshi TV show, 'You've Been Tamed'.

Your vision becomes technicoloured and blurry, like you're wearing 3-D Glasses with Rainbow Shades on top of them, and through this crazy vision you can just make out images of Dr Strangeglove flashing up in front of you, laughing evilly.

"Mwah, ha, ha, ha!"

"I should've known this had something to do with you, Strangeglove," you shout out, and then you realize you are no longer in control of yourself. You are being dragged away from the gallery by some sort of immense force and there is nothing you can do to stop it.

"I must have been completely hypnotized by the prints!" you gasp, annoyed at your over indulging and greediness. And then, **BANG!** Everything goes black . . .

You wake up in a dark cave that smells a little bit like a zoo. As your eyes become accustomed to the light, you see that you are surrounded by lots of little Moshlings.

"We're caught in a trap!" you scream, but all the Moshlings seem oblivious, like they are in some sort of trance.

You try to jump up and investigate your surroundings, but your hands are quite literally tied.

Luckily, you got a badge at Gout-Scout Camp for untying knots of any sort with your feet. You always knew it would come in handy. (Or should that be feety?)

You wait until Strangeglove is busy working on a machine on the other side of the cave, then untie yourself and all the Moshlings around you with your amazing tinkering toes. Searching along the slimy walls of the cave, you find a trapdoor to the Underground Tunnels, and send all the Moshlings through it. Luckily Strangeglove doesn't turn around until you have just about managed to squeeze the final fluffy hairs of your furry self through the door.

'Perhaps if I hadn't eaten so many of the prints, I would have been faster!' you say to yourself. But it doesn't matter, as you have escaped the dastardly Strangeglove in the nick of time.

You may not have solved the mystery of the art thief exactly, but when you get back to the Googenheim, you tell a team of Super Moshis everything you know. Your information proves vital in them tracking down Strangeglove and the missing paintings. Monstro City's art world has a lot to thank you, and in particular your feet for, so very well done!

THE END

Following on behind a big group of Moshlings, you realize your vision is still really hazy from the mist in the gallery. You pull out Zack Binspin's Eau de Trash Perfume and spray it into your eyes. It hurts and we don't advise you ever do this again, but it works, and your vision begins to clear.

You start to see that you are not in a dream world or theme park at all, but some sort of dingy underground cave full of traps and contraptions to glump Moshlings!

You see eye-fried Moshlings thinking they are having fun in the Hall of Mirrors, but actually they are heading to their doom.

The Moshlings on the Ferris wheel may be screaming with joy right now, but if they knew they were actually on a water wheel leading them to a machine that will glump them, they would be screaming with fear.

"Thank goodness I didn't go on the wheel," you think, relieved.

You see more Moshlings so hypnotized that they are walking up never-ending staircases, probably thinking they are having the time of their lives and not realizing they are actually creating energy to power the machines that will bring their eventual doom.

The Eye C U Goo and its potent mist has permanently hypnotized them. You try spraying more of your perfume around you, but it doesn't seem to be strong enough.

"They must have been exposed to too much of the goo!"

You walk all the way to the other side of the cave

and find Dr. Strangeglove about to press a very big and important-looking button, with the word 'GLUMP!' on it.

You think quickly and use your F-f-funky Door to bend time and space and freeze Dr Strangeglove to the spot. It's only going to hold for a few minutes, but it should give you enough time to do one of two things.

You can see an enormous bucket full of Eye C U Goo to the left of Strangeglove up on a shelf. You could give him a taste of his own medicine and tip that on him, hypnotize him and force him to believe he is on his very own favourite fairground ride.

Or, you could call on a team of Super Moshis to evacuate the Moshlings from the whole place, whilst you deactivate the wiring on the glumping button?

If you pour the bucket load of Eye C U Goo over Strangeglove, **turn to page 60.**

If you evacuate the Moshlings and deactivate the button, **turn to page 72.**

Putting the Mystery Box to one side, you spray and spray and spray the Colorama paint, trying out as many different colour combos as you can.

"Smudgetastic rainbows, there are a monstrous amount of combinations to try!" you gasp. But this doesn't stop you from taking the time to look in the mirror at each and every one.

Just as you are admiring combo number 315 – an aqua fur-coat, with sunshine yellow fur tips, purplelicious eyes and ruby red lips – the gorgeous Tyra Fangs walks in. You have never actually seen her in the real monster flesh before, but you've heard lots about her. She's a runway model, TV show host, and gossip queen. She originally comes from the fashion capital, Goo York, but now spends her days in Monstro City. She is definitely an awesome M-List celeb spot!

"Yo, Tyra," you say, trying to act cool and calm, but you are secretly very excited about meeting an actual M-List celebrity.

"Loving your style, Moshi!" she replies.

You point at yourself, as if to say, 'who, me?'

Tyra picks up your furry body language. "Of course, you. There's no one else around is there?"

You are completely embarrassed and your aqua fur-coat mixes with a touch of pink in your embarrassment, creating a whole new fashion statement.

You begin chatting to Tyra about the latest looks in monster chic and get on with her like a Haunted House on fire. You completely forget about your mission at hand – which, by the way, is finding the art thief!

The next day, Tyra whisks you off into the Moshi fashion world, where your individual style is well received on the cool as a cat-walk.

You never do find the art thief, but life isn't too bad, as you love your new modelling career! Fashion is art after all, my darling!

On your next flight to Goo York you read the latest issue of Monstro City's *Vague* magazine. There's an article about how the Super Moshis had found out that Dr. Strangeglove had stolen the paintings and replaced them with forgeries to entice Moshlings to his Glumping machine. Luckily they were saved in the nick of time. It could have been you, so maybe you could try being a detective again, after you're done with your swanky new fashion career?

THE END

Heading down the tunnel, the light gets brighter and brighter and you see the footprints on the ground again. There seem to be two different types of prints, one pair of little ones, and one bigger set.

"Maybe the art thief is actually art thieves, and I'm looking for a team working together?" you wonder.

Just as your thoughts begin to drift off into likely teams of suspects, you notice a pile of sparkling Rox on the floor. You bend over to pick them up.

"Grrr!" you growl, trying desperately to pick up each one, but all of the Rox seem to be well and truly stuck to the floor.

"GRRR!" you growl, louder, trying harder than before. But it's no use, the Rox just won't budge.

Despite no one being around, you still feel slightly embarrassed by trying to pick up the Rox, so you continue to walk along, pretending like nothing has happened, whistling a happy tune.

Soon, you come to a door. You open it up and walk through . . .

SPLAT! You are covered in what looks, feels and tastes like Toad Soda, made from real toads. "Well at least I don't have to change my clothes, as I don't have any!" you say, trying to smile through the mess.

Thinking about your missing clothes and the random events that have been happening to you all day – the banana skin on the floor you tripped over, the crowd ready to cheer for you, the judges marking your swinging technique, the Rox stuck on the floor to torment you, and now the Toad Soda all too conveniently placed above a door you have to walk through – it's all beginning to feel like a bit of a strange coincidence.

"It must be someone trying to trick me," you say. "Someone who likes playing practical jokes. Or some people, as there are two sets of footprints?"

You rack your brains for notorious Monstro City practical jokers.

"Aha, it must be the silent yet violent joking scoundrels, Bug and Ratty!" you exclaim. "I'd bet 100 Rox on the fact that they stole the Old Masters and this whole thing is one great big wind up. After all, they are always up to some sort of mischief." You'd even heard that the terrible trickstering two had rearranged the dino bones over at the Unnatural History Museum, causing chaos and confusion.

But then you start having second thoughts, "Surely stealing all those paintings is a little bit extreme, even for them? After all, they are so little, how would they have been able to carry them all away?"

If you decide that all this must have something to do with Bug and Ratty, **turn to page 22.**

If you decide it has nothing to do with Bug and Ratty, **turn to page 31.**

You're a little bit nervous about heading straight into a Super Moshi mission, so training is best for you. Besides preparing you to hunt down the art thief, you should make some great new buddies.

You're taken to a chamber beneath the Volcano, labelled 'TOP SECRET Train-in-Room – Keep Out'.

The sign is right – you open the small door and see an actual train in the room in front of you! This is not what you'd thought they meant by train-in!

Taking everything in your stride, like only a Super Moshi would, you keep calm and await further instructions.

You are told to board the train in the driver's carriage and take the hot seat, which is almost as hot as your Fried Egg Rug! But you do as you're told anyway, and a control panel and screen lights up in front of you, as your bottom sizzles away on the seat.

Next, you are given some advice: keep your wits about you, trust your instincts and react as quickly and as safely as you can.

A flashing green, 'GO!' appears on the screen, and you find yourself looking at Dr. Strangeglove carrying some sort of chemical powder over to a tank full of Fishies. It doesn't look like fish food to you and you realize your mission must be to stop him.

You must choose from the following equipment to solve the task: Amazon Warrior Tiara, Nutz and Boltz Chair or Electronic Tickling Arm.

"Go, Electronic Tickling Arm!" you shout out, and

an arm appears in front of you with a handful of Birdies feathers and tickles Strangeglove on the nose.

"At-choo!" sneezes Strangeglove, and the power of his sneeze causes the powder to fly everywhere.

"Woohoo!" you cheer, realizing you made the right choice.

Strangeglove turns away from you and begins to run. The train engine splutters and starts up and you now have to chase him around Monstro City, using the steering wheel and control panel. It's pretty hair-raising, so every bit of your fur stands on end!

You soon catch up with Strangeglove and manage to lead him to the edge of The Port, but you don't know how to stop the train before you reach the water!

"Yikes!"

Both the aqua blue and fiery orange buttons are flashing away on the panel in front of you, but you don't feel like you've been given any clues as to what to do next. Which one should you press?

If you press the aqua blue button, **turn to page 17.**

If you press the fiery orange button, **turn to page 44.**

57

You climb aboard the Ferris wheel and start spinning around and around.

"Aha!" you cry, spotting Strangeglove on the other side of the Moshi Fun Park, herding dazed and confused Moshlings into some sort of contraption. "I must get over there."

You press the eject button, but the wheel won't stop. Just then, you begin to realize . . .

"The mist from the gunk in the gallery must be in my eyes and it's making me see things!"

You frantically de-mist your eyes, by spraying your Eau de Trash Perfume all over yourself.

"It worked!" you cheer. Looking around, you see that you are not on a Ferris wheel, but some sort of water wheel, leading to a Moshling glumping machine!

"All the rides must be illusions and traps!" you gasp, horrified. "This Moshling 'dream world' is actually a 'nightmare world', where Strangeglove is turning all the Moshlings into glumps!"

You remember your F-f-funky Door, whip it out and use it to bend time and space and stop the wheel in its spinning tracks.

Knowing that time will only be bent for a few minutes, you quickly scale your way down the wheel, jump down to the floor and land right in a pile of extremely super sticky gum from the Bazaar's Gumball Machine!

"Yuck!" you gasp. Then you realize that your sticky situation is actually just what you need. You prise the gum off and use it to stick the cogs of the wheel together and hold it in place for longer. You clamber up and rescue all the Moshlings from the wheel and their impending doom!

The next day you find out that while you were busy saving the Moshlings on the wheel from their watery glumping end, a team of Super Moshis on the other side of the Fun Park used Strangeglove's goo to hypnotize him, while they released the rest of the Moshlings. Good team work, Super Moshis!

THE END

Whilst Strangeglove is frozen in motion, you head over to the enormous bucket of Eye C U Goo and lever it off the shelf with a plank. It slowly creaks up and over, and you tip the entire contents onto him.

You call on your fellow Super Moshis to help you gather up the Moshlings and get them out of the cave quickly.

You search around for the original Old and Mouldy Masters paintings, and find them just in time to hear,

"ARGGGHHH!" Strangeglove is stirring from his frozen state, as the F-f-funky Door effect is wearing off. He moves his hand away from the button and starts walking straight towards you. Just before he walks into you, he suddenly turns left!

'He must be heading to his favourite dream world!' you think to yourself, amused that your roles have been reversed and you leave him to get on with it! You're sure he'll find a way to escape the state, but everyone is safe for now, at least.

You return the Old and Mouldy Masters to the Googenheim and then buy every last bottle of Zack Binspin's perfume and use it to stop the Moshlings from being hypnotized any longer.

You solving the Great Googenheist is headline news in the *Daily Growl* the next day, and you now have a permanent grin of pride on your face – not unlike the *Monsta Lisa* herself!

THE END

With your hands still in the air from your 'Do The Funky Monster' moves, you quickly grab hold of the Colorama's paint blasters without any of the Super Moshis noticing you. You direct them at the team, then press GO!

Splurt, splurt, splutter, splutter! The paint trickles out of the blasters, into a little pool right in front of you and nowhere near the Super Moshis.

"Oh no!" you cry. "So much for blasting them. I must have used up all the paint."

You scramble around trying to find some more paint pots and change the colours in the machine, but the Super Moshis are all back on their feet and surround you.

"I'm afraid you'll have to come with us," they tell you, escorting you out of the Colorama Workshop.

They take you back to the Googenheim and question you. You're hoping that finally you'll have a chance to explain everything, plead your innocence and maybe even help the team of Super Moshis find the real art thief.

But despite all the questions, you still can't really explain why it was exactly that you were in the Googenheim today, when you've never been there before. Or why today just happened to be the day that the forgeries were found. Or the fact that your paw, teeth and even nose prints were found all over the crime scene. Surely, if you were just investigating the scene, you would have just taken a sample of the prints or used gloves like Inspector Clueless would have done?

When you explain that you then went to the Colorama

Workshop to find more clues, the Super Moshis accuse you of going there to lose the evidence. They say you were disguising the fact that you are the only Moshi in the whole of Monstro City whose paw prints exactly match the colour of those in the gallery!

"We caught you just before you destroyed the evidence," they say. "If you were innocent, you never would have tried to blast us with the paint and escape."

That night, the Super Moshis search your house and garden, and can't find the real paintings anywhere. Obviously you are not surprised and can't help them. You'd love to know where they are more than anything else in the whole of Monstro City right now!

"Until you tell us where they are, we're going to keep you imprisoned in one of the paintings in the gallery," explains Super Katsuma, "so we know where 'thou art' at all times!"

'They sure do love their jokes,' you think.

So they choose one of the fake Old Masters, (a blue one of course, so you match) and stick you into it with the toughest, stickiest stuff of all time – Super Glooper Glue, and put you on the wall for all to see. What little reputation and dignity you have is ruined!

Days later, after further, and more thorough, investigations by the Super Moshis, they find out that you have been used as a decoy by the real art thief, Dr. Strangeglove.

But they're too late. You're already stuck in the painting and will have to stay there until they find something that can break down the immense strength of the Super Glooper Glue!

"It must've been something to do with the paw prints you say, maybe I should never have tasted the gunk? Perhaps this was all a trap?"

Whatever the answer, all you know for sure is that you have, quite literally, been FRAMED!!!

THE END

With your Reading Glasses and Actual-Magnifying Glass in toe, (well in 'hand' really, but that's not really the point is it?) you take a closer look at the forgeries.

The curator was right, they were great copies, although having never actually seen the real ones yourself, you have to trust him on that one. You take a look at the signatures.

"Van . . . Goop . . . Gok," you read from the new version of Van Goo Goo's *Sunshine Berries*. "Well, from this I can conclude that, although the thief seems to be able to paint well, his or her spelling sure ain't too good!"

You go through all the forgeries and find a number of spelling mistakes and grammatical errors. You realize that your fascination with the signatures may impress Roary Scrawl, but it isn't going to get you any closer to finding the art thief. So you try something else . . .

Seeing that the paint is STILL wet, you work out that it cannot possibly be normal paint and that the substance itself needs further investigation.

"Even Oily Boily Paint would've dried by now," you say, thinking hard.

You head over to the paw prints on the wall that you had noticed earlier on. Using the Actual-Magnifying Glass to make a couple of the prints larger than they actually are, you try to see if the paint itself can give you any clues as to the thief, and where they might have come from.

You can see the substance is thick and made up of all sorts of colours, despite generally looking quite blue.

"I actually don't think I've ever seen this colour before!" you exclaim, surprised.

Suddenly you realise that the paw prints appear to be more like glove prints! There are no actual finger or paw marks so you must assume that the thief was wearing gloves. The only Moshi you know who wears gloves all the time, even on a hot day like today, is the scientific genius and former Doctor of Moshlingology himself . . .

"Dr Strangeglove!" you shout out.

"Where?!" gasps everyone around you in horror.

"Nowhere, sorry," you reply sheepishly. You hadn't meant to cause any alarm, so you put your head down and get back to work.

Could this really be the work of Strangeglove? The thief could obviously paint, and although Strangeglove was an expert at many things, you don't think it's likely that painting beautiful gruesome paintings was really going to be one of those things. Surely he was too busy trying to take over Monstro City to have time to paint pictures? So you think again . . . there were mysterious artists you had heard of who, it was reported in the *Daily Growl*, liked not only to paint, but also to pull stunts and jokes on the Moshis of Monstro City. You could just about recall one of their names,

"Art Lee!" you shout out.

"Where?!" gasps everyone around you, intrigued this time.

"Nowhere. Sorry. Again," you reply, almost in a whisper.

You keep thinking, then quietly say to yourself, "As a mysterious amateur graffiti artist, Art Lee has been working towards becoming the next Danksy. Although he spends most of his time in the Underground Caves, creating super-sweet works of pop art, he could have come up for a bit, used gloves to create some kind of Pop Art statement on the Old and Mouldy Masters, and made it look like a crime had been committed by Strangeglove, disguising his identity at the same time."

"Are you talking to yourself?" a young Dino Moshling asks you, running up towards the prints.

You've been so busy looking closely at the prints, you haven't even noticed that an enormous group of Moshlings are now following the paw prints in front of you, as if they are in some sort of trance. They seem absolutely obsessed with them.

'How odd,' you think. Then, your mind goes back to the conundrum, Art Lee or Dr. Strangeglove? The question whirls around in your mind and you find yourself constantly jumping from one to the other, like a Moshi in desperate need of the bathroom, hopping from one leg to another!

All this tossing and turning from one conclusion to the next has your brain totally puzzled out! Are you really cut out for this investigative larking about? Weigh up your options and prove that you are, by deciding what your next steps will be . . .

If you decide to head underground and investigate
the underground art world or Art Lee,
turn to page 11.

If you decide the glove prints must be from
Strangeglove and want to enlist the help of
Elder Furi, **turn to page 74.**

Dragging yourself away from the yummy prints, you race out of the Googenheim, down Ooh La Lane, over the bridge and on to The Port.

"One of the first rules of being a detective is to leave no stones unturned," you say to yourself, remembering more of Inspector Clueless' wise words, "and to question everyone you meet on the street. You never know how they may be able to help."

So, after turning over every stone, rock and boulder you can find, including poor old Myrtle the Diving Turtle (who was just trying to snooze after her latest treasure hunt), you decide to interrogate everyone you meet, to see if you can find any more clues.

First you spot Gail Whale. Well she's hard to miss, as she is as big as a whale after all!

"Gail!" you holler out across Potion Ocean. "Have you seen anything fishy going on around these parts?"

"Of course I have," replies Gail. "I have something fishy for breakfast, lunch and dinner, so there's always something fishy going on round here."

"OK, thanks Gail," you shout back, not really meaning it, and turn your attention to Roland Jones, who is sitting right by you. Roland always seems to be hanging out at The Port. He must have seen something, surely?

"So, Roland," you begin, but Roland just rolls away from you. His obsession with Wobble Ade, and thinking that it will make him grow as big as his brother and sisters seems to have taken its toll, and he just can't keep still!

"Well, he's about as useful as a wobbly Crab and Jelly Sandwich," you sigh, looking up at the sky.

"SQUAWK!" squawks Patch the Seagull, as he nose dives towards you from a great height.

You duck out of the way just in time, before he lands right on your head!

Patch monitors The Port for unsavoury characters and scraps of leftovers from the fishermen, so maybe, just maybe, he may be able to help with your investigation.

"Hi there, Patch," you say. "Have you noticed any funny business going on at the Port lately?"

"Nothing more than usual," replies Patch. "I mean, there was a monster with a truck load of paint–" but before finishing his sentence, Patch is distracted by something and flies, up, up and away out of sight.

"Paaaatch!" you shout, but it's too late. He's gone.

Finally, you decide to give up on witnesses and make a quick stop at Paws 'n' Claws, to pick up a Mystery Box for clues. Then you enter the colour-tastic world of the Colorama Workshop.

"Now then, where to start?" you ask, looking around the room full of paint splodges and goo. None of it looks, smells, feels, sounds or tastes like the prints from the Googenheim.

"Maybe, if I mix a few of the paints together, I'll find the right combination and get that strange colour I saw in the gallery?" you ask yourself.

"This colour combo thing is great!" you giggle, spraying

yourself with all the colours of the rainbow and admiring yourself in the mirror. "I could keep going all day!"

Just then, you remember you've forgotten to check inside your Mystery Box for a clue. You open it up and find a riddle inside:

I'm often wet and not so dry,
I can be high up in the sky.
I'm in berry, and denim too,
Stick with me and you won't feel _____!

"Blue!" you gasp, believing you have cracked the code. "Maybe I should use all the blues to make a new blue, and make myself entirely blue so I'll match the thief?"

But then, you have second thoughts. The prints weren't a blue you've ever seen before, so maybe they weren't blue at all, but another new colour, not yet created?

What are you going to do?

If you decide to keep trying out different colours and combos to find a new colour, that has never been seen before, **turn to page 52.**

If you decide to trust the Mystery Box and follow the blue clue (Fablo Fiasco has spent so much time using the colour blue after all), **turn to page 18**.

At least no one in the Underground Tunnels knows your true identity or why you went there in the first place. And that's how you would like to keep it for now, thank you very much.

THE END

You call upon your fellow Super Moshis and they evacuate the Moshlings, whilst you head over to the 'GLUMP!' button.

You look at the wiring and see that you have the choice of two wires to pull out, a red one and a black one.

"Not another decision," you sigh, but Strangeglove is beginning to twitch and you're worried that the effects of the F-f-funky Door are going to wear off any minute.

"Here goes!" you shout, as you yank both the red and the black wire out of their connections!

Luckily, the flashing stops and it appears to have worked. You have successfully deactivated the button.

"Electric Apricots!" you yell, excitedly.

You have just enough time left over to tie up Strangeglove and find all the Old and Mouldy Masters, before time and space is back to normal again. He wakes up, but the rope you tied him up with holds him until you slip away from the cave.

You return the original paintings to the Googenheim, destroy the forgeries, clean off the prints and return the Moshlings to the Moshling Garden, whilst you work on an antidote for the side effects of them being hypnotized in the Super Moshi lab.

"Phew! What a day!" you gasp, collapsing into bed that night.

With reports on your heroism in the *Daily Growl* the next day, you realize it's all been worth it. You may not be an infamous Old Master, but you sure did paint a good picture of yourself to the monsters of Monstro City!

THE END

Picking up the conical flask, you shut your eyes and throw the entire contents of the Eye C U Goo Smoothie down your throat. Despite your previous best efforts to make it taste better, by adding some salt and hot pepper, it does not taste nice. Not at all!

Just five seconds later you find yourself standing on a big bridge, before you're being pushed into some sort of Hot Smelly-Air Balloon, powered (in part) by gas from Roland Jones' Wobble Ade burps. It carries you over the glorious heights of Monstro City and far, far, away, then drops you off in the Moshi Fun Park

"I love it here!" you say, smiling and seeing all your favourite theme park rides, favourite food stalls and favourite Moshis – all in one fantastic place.

The sky is blue, the sun is shining yellow and there's a glorious rainbow sparkling. You can see you are surrounded by lots of little Moshlings, but you have completely forgotten about the art thief and that you are there to save them. Instead you spend your days having fun on the rides, oblivious.

You are completely wrapped up in your own colourful dream world, you couldn't have painted a more perfect picture of life! The only way you'll ever escape is if Elder Furi realizes you are missing and sends his top team of Super Moshis to find you. But to be honest, there's no rush, there are many worse ways to spend your time!

THE END

Convinced that the paw-prints are unquestionably the work of the most infamous gloved one in Monstro City, Dr. Strangeglove, you know the only way you'll have any chance of tracking him down, is by enlisting the help of Elder Furi and the Super Moshis.

"I need to head to the Volcano," you say. "That seems to be the place everyone heads to for their Super Moshi missions."

So you race off to Main Street, but in front of Yukea, you notice something strange going on.

"I'm sure Lila Tweet and Pete Slurp are usually over there having a picnic," you say, confused, as they are nowhere to be seen. Instead Sly Chance is creeping around, looking extremely, well sly, really.

'How odd,' you think to yourself, with your hand on your chin like a thoughtful detective, 'I'm sure that shady Sly is only ever wheelin' and dealin' over at Dodgy Dealz. What is he up to over here?'

You know that Sly must be up to no good of some sort, and think he may have been trying to make some quick Rox by selling the original Old and Mouldy Monsterpiece paintings from the Googenheim on the street.

If you decide to talk to Sly Chance and see what he's up to, **turn to page 36.**

If you decide to ignore Sly and continue on your journey to find Elder Furi, **turn to page 25.**

You race back to the lab to see if you can save some of the Eye C U Goo from your experiments.

You fling on your Super Moshi lab coat again and set to work, trying to salvage what you can of the remaining Goo.

But all you can scrape together are some little blobs here and there, and they are pretty watered down and weak.

You stare long and hard at the weak Goo, but nothing seems to be happening. So you keep staring and staring at it, for longer and longer, hoping for some sort of hypnotism or illusion that has been taking the Moshlings away.

"Oooh!" you gasp, starting to see lots of dots in front of you, some bigger than others. Then they disappear and you realize you're just staring at a Polka Dot Dress someone has left hanging up in the cloakroom.

"Aaah!" you gasp, seeing a beautiful field. "Now I must be hypnotized!" The field is full of Smiley Flowers and an enormous picnic of one of your favourite foods, Bangers and Mash, sits in the middle of it.

But soon, the mirage disappears and you find yourself back in the lab.

"That little illusion of my dream place and food is not going to be good enough for me to find the location of the Moshlings and Strangeglove," you sigh.

You put your thinking hat on, which looks a lot like an Aussie Fly Hat, but with fewer flies, and decide that the best thing you can do is make an Eye C U Goo Smoothie and drink it.

"That way, I'll get the most concentrated form of the

Eye C U Goo," you say. You whip up the smoothie in the conical flask, and it actually looks surprisingly appetising. You would not recommend anyone ever try this at home themselves, but in a time of total crisis, you realize you have no choice.

But you do have a choice: should you take just a little sip, or drink down the whole lot?

If you just take a sip of the smoothie,
turn to page 14.

If you guzzle down the entire contents of the conical flask, **turn to page 73.**

You ignore the Moshi in the cape. "He could just be someone pretending to be a Super Moshi, sent here to trick me and make me go off course," you say, suspiciously.

You walk towards the lava flowing into the moat and hop very carefully from rock to rock, over the wickedly hot molten pools.

"Flaming Lava Lamps!" you scream nervously, as you only just make it to the other side without wobbling over!

You walk through the grand door and down some stairs and find yourself in a big round room, bursting with masked Moshis busily racing around trying to go on missions. You're completely surrounded by television and computer screens, flashing lights and Rox. It's like a complete energy overload, and the nerves about what you are here to do send a shiver down your tail!

"Welcome," says a voice from above.

"Thank you," you reply, almost jumping out of your furry skin!

"Now then, young Moshi. I know why it is that you are here and I need to tell you that you have two choices."

"OK," you reply, listening very carefully.

The wise one explains that the art thief must be found very quickly and that you can either take part in detective training in a simulator, or go straight to a lab to investigate with a top team of Super Moshis.

"So what do you decide to do first, young Super Moshi in training?" asks Elder Furi. "You must make your decision quickly. We don't have much time."

So quick, get deciding . . .

If you decide to try the simulator first to prepare yourself, **turn to page 56.**

If you decide to take the plunge and go furry head over heels into the mission at hand and head to the lab, **turn to page 46.**

The TOP SECRET file is very informative, so you're pretty glad you chose to use it for the next part of your investigation.

"Whoever stole the paintings must be trying to sell them and make zillions of Rox," you say, "or they never would have taken them in the first place. That means that they must be in a shop somewhere in Monstro City."

You head out of the gallery and down the slope, this time avoiding any obstacles that may make you slide. When you get to the exit, you notice a box that looks like a present, but you ignore it.

"It's probably just another trick being played on me," you assume, leaving without a backwards glance.

"First stop, Horrods!" you command, as if you have a team of Moshis following you, but it's simply you and you alone, as pretty much everyone in Monstro City has flocked to the Googenheim to find out what's going on there. Horrods is in the TOP SECRET file as the number one place for selling expensive paintings, so it should definitely be your first point of call.

"Hello there, Mizz Snoots," you say. "Do you have any paintings to sell?"

"I'm afraid I don't, but I do have . . ."

Mizz Snoots trails off and before you know it, you find yourself buying a number of extravagant items, including: a Fountain, Spider Chandelier, Tesla Lamp, Shakesfear Bust, Iron Furnace and the Platinum Pants of Power – Possessing Platinum Pants Proves Power, which you are told to purchase promptly!

Now you have the shopping bug and there is like nothing you can do about it, girlfriend! You forget all about the investigation and race around the city, buying everything you can lay your hands on. You are totally out of control!

Exhausted from your day of shopping, and none the wiser as to who the art thief is, you head home.

"Oh well," you sigh contentedly, leaping into your comfy and brand new bed, "I'm sure I'll read all about it in the *Daily Growl* tomorrow, all snuggled up on my gorgeous new Sausage Sofa!"

THE END